# The HUG Book

By **Sue Fliess**

Illustrated by **Anne Kennedy**

## A GOLDEN BOOK · NEW YORK

Text copyright © 2015 by Sue Fliess
Illustrations copyright © 2015 by Anne Kennedy
All rights reserved. Published in the United States by Golden Books, an imprint of Random House Children's Books, a division of Random House LLC, 1745 Broadway, New York, NY 10019, and in Canada by Random House of Canada Limited, Toronto, Penguin Random House Companies. Golden Books, A Golden Book, A Little Golden Book, the G colophon, and the distinctive gold spine are registered trademarks of Random House LLC.
randomhousekids.com
Educators and librarians, for a variety of teaching tools, visit us at
RHTeachersLibrarians.com
Library of Congress Control Number: 2013946579
ISBN 978-0-385-37907-6 (trade) — ISBN 978-0-375-98228-6 (ebook)
Printed in the United States of America
10 9 8 7 6 5 4 3

**U**nder covers, nice and snug.
Ready for a morning hug?

Mom hugs,
Dad hugs,
No-such-thing-as-bad hugs!

Old hugs,

New hugs,
Nice-to-see-you-too hugs!

Greet hugs,
Sweet hugs,
Sweep-you-off-your-feet hugs.

Leg hugs,
Shy hugs,

Thanks-for-stopping-by hugs.

"Why?" hugs,
Cry hugs,
Hard-to-say-goodbye hugs.

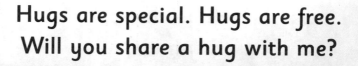

Hugs are special. Hugs are free.
Will you share a hug with me?

Soft hugs,
Pet hugs,
Take-her-to-the-vet hugs.

Five hugs,
Ten hugs,
Welcome-home-again hugs.

Clean hugs,
Wet hugs,
Here I come to get hugs!

Big hugs,
Tall hugs,
Travel-down-the-hall hugs.

Good hugs,
Night hugs,